SECRET WORSHIP

BY

ALGERNON BLACKWOOD

British Library Cataloguing-in-Publication Data
A catalogue record for this book is available from
the British Library

Contents

ALGERNON BLACKWOOD

Algernon Henry Blackwood was born in Shooter's Hill, South East England, in 1869. In his youth he trained as a doctor at Wellington College in Berkshire, and went on to pursue a number of careers, in areas as varied as milk farming, modelling, journalism and violin teaching. In his thirties, Blackwood returned to England from New York, where he had spent a number of years, and began to write stories of the supernatural.

Blackwood was extremely prolific, producing over the course of his life some ten original collections of short stories, fourteen novels, several children's books, and a number of plays. Most of his work was concerned with the ghostly, mythical or occult – themes which Blackwood was attracted to his whole life – and he is regarded as one of the earlier practitioners of 'weird fiction'. Amongst his best known short stories are 'The Wendigo', and 'The Willows' – a work which H. P. Lovecraft called "the finest weird story I have ever read." In 1914, he produced his short story collection *Incredible Adventures*, which leading literary critic

S. T. Joshi has said "may be the premier weird collection of this or any other century." Blackwood worked as an undercover agent for Britain during the First World War, and during the 1920s became famous for reading his ghost stories live on BBC radio and television.

After a number of strokes, Blackwood died in old age in Kent, England.

Secret Worship

Algernon Blackwood

———————

HARRIS, THE SILK merchant, was in South Germany on his way home from a business trip when the idea came to him suddenly that he would take the mountain railway from Strasbourg and run down to revisit his old school after an interval of something more than thirty years. And it was to this chance impulse of the junior partner in Harris Brothers of St Paul's Churchyard that John Silence owed one of the most curious cases of his whole experience, for at that very moment he happened to be tramping these same mountains with a holiday knapsack, and from different points of the compass the two men were actually converging towards the same inn.

Deep down in the heart that for thirty years had been concerned chiefly with the profitable buying and selling of silk Harris's school had left the imprint of its peculiar influence and, though perhaps unknown to Harris, had strongly coloured the whole of his subsequent existence. It belonged to the deeply religious life of a small Protestant community (which it is unnecessary to specify), and his father had sent him there at the age of fifteen, partly because he would learn the German requisite for the conduct of the silk business, and partly because the discipline was strict, and discipline was what his soul and body needed just then more than anything else.

The life, indeed, had proved exceedingly severe, and young Harris benefited accordingly; for though corporal punishment was unknown, there was a system of mental and spiritual correction which somehow made the soul stand proudly erect to receive it, while it struck at the very root of the fault and taught the boy that his character was being cleaned and strengthened, and that he was not merely being tortured in a kind of personal revenge.

That was over thirty years ago, when he was a dreamy and impressionable youth of fifteen; and now, as the train climbed slowly up the winding mountain gorges, his mind travelled back somewhat lovingly over the intervening period, and forgotten details rose vividly again before him out of the shadows. The life there had been very wonderful, it seemed to him, in that remote mountain village, protected from the tumults of the world by the love and worship of the devout Brotherhood that ministered to the needs of some hundred boys from every country in Europe. Sharply the scenes came back to him. He smelt again the long stone corridors, the hot pinewood rooms, where the sultry hours of summer study were passed with bees droning through open windows in the sunshine, and German characters struggling in the mind with dreams of English lawns – and then the sudden awful cry of the master in German –

'Harris, stand up! You sleep!'

And he recalled the dreadful standing motionless for an hour, book in hand, while the knees felt like wax and the head grew heavier than a cannonball.

The very smell of the cooking came back to him – the daily *Sauerkraut*, the watery chocolate on Sundays, the flavour of the stringy meat served twice a week at *Mittagessen*; and he smiled to think again of the half-rations that was the punishment for speaking English. The very odour of the milk-bowls – the hot sweet aroma that rose from the soaking peasant-bread at the six o'clock breakfast – came back to him pungently, and he saw the huge *Speisesaal* with the hundred boys in their school uniform, all eating sleepily in silence, gulping down the coarse bread and scalding milk in terror of the bell that would presently cut them short – and, at the far end where the masters sat, he saw the narrow slit windows with the vistas of enticing field and forest beyond.

And this, in turn, made him think of the great barn-like room on the top floor where all slept together in wooden cots, and he heard in memory the clamour of the cruel bell that woke them on winter mornings at five o'clock and summoned them to the stone-flagged *Waschkammer*, where boys and masters alike, after scanty and icy washing, dressed in complete silence.

From this his mind passed swiftly, with vivid picture-thoughts, to other things, and with a passing shiver he remembered how the loneliness of never being alone had eaten into him, and how everything – work, meals, sleep, walks, leisure – was done with his 'division' of twenty other boys and under the eyes of at least two masters. The only solitude possible was by asking for half an hour's practice in the cell-like music rooms, and Harris smiled to himself as he recalled the zeal of his violin studies.

Then, as the train puffed laboriously through the great pine forests that cover these mountains with a giant carpet of velvet, he found the pleasanter layers of memory giving up their dead, and he recalled with admiration the kindness of the masters, whom all addressed as Brother, and marvelled afresh at their devotion in burying themselves for years in such a place, only to leave it, in most cases, for the still rougher life of missionaries in the wild places of the world.

He thought once more of the still, religious atmosphere that hung over the little forest community like a veil, barring the distressful world; of the picturesque ceremonies at Easter, Christmas, and New Year; of the numerous feast-days and charming little festivals. The *Beschehr-Fest*, in particular, came back to him – the feast of gifts at Christmas – when the entire community paired off and gave presents, many of which had taken weeks to make or the savings of many days to purchase. And then he saw the midnight ceremony in the church at New Year, with the shining face of the *Prediger* in the pulpit – the village preacher who, on the last night of the old year, saw in the empty gallery beyond the organ loft the faces of all who were to die in the ensuing twelve months, and who at last recognised himself among them, and, in the very middle of his sermon, passed into a state of rapt ecstasy and burst into a torrent of praise.

Thickly the memories crowded upon him. The picture of the small village dreaming its unselfish life on the mountain tops, clean, wholesome, simple, searching vigorously for its God, and training hundreds of boys in the grand way, rose up in his mind with all the power of an obsession. He felt once more the old mystical enthusiasm, deeper than the sea and more wonderful than the stars; he heard again the winds sighing from leagues of forest over the red roofs in the moonlight; he heard the Brothers' voices talking of the things beyond this life as though they had actually experienced them in the body; and, as he sat in the jolting train, a spirit of unutterable longing passed over his seared and tired soul, stirring in the depths of him a sea of emotions that he thought had long since frozen into immobility.

And the contrast pained him – the idealistic dreamer then, the man of business now – so that a spirit of unworldly peace and beauty known only to the soul in meditation laid its feathered finger upon his heart, moving strangely the surface of the waters.

Harris shivered a little and looked out of the window of his empty carriage. The train had long passed Hornberg, and far below the streams tumbled in white foam down the limestone rocks. In front of him, dome upon dome of wooded mountain stood against the sky. It was October, and the air was cool and sharp, wood-smoke and damp moss exquisitely mingled in it with the subtle odours of the pines. Overhead, between the tips of the highest firs, he saw the first stars peeping, and the sky was a clean, pale amethyst that seemed exactly the colour all these memories clothed themselves with in his mind.

He leaned back in his corner and sighed. He was a heavy man, and he had not known sentiment for years; he was a big man, and it took much to move him, literally and figuratively; he was a man in whom the dreams of God that haunt the soul in youth, though overlaid by the scum that gathers in the fight for money, had not, as with the majority, utterly died the death.

He came back into this little neglected pocket of the years where so much fine gold had collected and lain undisturbed, with all his semi-spiritual emotions aquiver; and, as he watched the mountain tops come nearer, and smelt the forgotten odours of his boyhood, something melted on the surface of his soul and left him sensitive to a degree he had not known since, thirty years before, he had lived here with his dreams, his conflicts, and his youthful suffering.

A thrill ran through him as the train stopped with a jolt at a tiny station and he saw the name in large black lettering on the grey stone building, and below it, the number of metres it stood above the level of the sea.

'The highest point on the line!' he exclaimed. 'How well I remember it – Sommerau – Summer Meadow. The very next station is mine!'

And, as the train ran downhill with brakes on and steam shut off, he put his head out of the window and one by one saw the old familiar landmarks in the dusk. They stared at him like dead faces in a dream. Queer, sharp feelings, half poignant, half sweet, stirred in his heart.

'There's the hot, white road we walked along so often with the two Brüders always at our heels,' he thought; 'and there, by jove, is the turn through the forest to "*Die Galgen*", the stone gallows where they hanged the witches in olden days!'

He smiled a little as the train slid past.

'And there's the copse where the Lilies of the Valley powdered the ground in spring; and, I swear' – he put his head out with a sudden impulse – 'if that's not the very clearing where Calame, the French boy, chased the swallow-tail with me, and Brüder Pagel gave us half-rations for leaving the road without permission, and for shouting in our mother tongues!' And he laughed again as the memories came back with a rush, flooding his mind with vivid detail.

The train stopped, and he stood on the grey gravel platform like a man in a dream. It seemed half a century since he last waited there with corded wooden boxes, and got into the train for Strasbourg and home after the two years' exile. Time dropped from him like an old garment and he felt a boy again. Only, things looked so much smaller than his memory of them; shrunk and dwindled they looked, and the distances seemed on a curiously smaller scale.

He made his way across the road to the little Gasthaus, and, as he went, faces and figures of former schoolfellows – German, Swiss, Italian, French, Russian – slipped out of the shadowy woods and silently accompanied him. They flitted by his side, raising their eyes questioningly, sadly, to his. But their names he had forgotten. Some of the Brothers, too, came with them, and most of these he remembered by name – Brüder Röst, Brüder Pagel, Brüder Schliemann, and the bearded face of the old preacher who had seen himself in the haunted gallery of those about to die – Brüder Gysin. The dark forest lay all about him like a sea that any moment might rush with velvet waves upon the scene and sweep all the faces away. The air was cool and wonderfully fragrant, but with every perfumed breath came also a pallid memory. . . .

Yet, in spite of the underlying sadness inseparable from such an experience, it was all very interesting, and held a pleasure peculiarly its own, so that Harris engaged his room and ordered supper feeling well pleased with himself, and intending to walk up to the old school that very evening. It stood in the centre of the community's village, some four miles distant through the forest, and he now recollected for the first time that this little Protestant settlement dwelt isolated in a section of the country that was otherwise Catholic. Crucifixes and shrines surrounded the clearing like the sentries of a beleaguering army. Once beyond the square of the village, with its few acres of field and orchard, the forest crowded up in solid phalanxes, and beyond the rim of trees began the country that was ruled by the priests of another faith. He vaguely remembered, too, that the Catholics had showed sometimes a certain hostility toward the little Protestant oasis that flourished so quietly and benignly in their midst. He had quite forgotten this. How trumpery it all seemed now with his wide experience of life and his knowledge of other countries and the great outside world! It was like stepping back, not thirty years, but three hundred.

There were only two others besides himself at supper. One of them, a bearded, middle-aged man in tweeds, sat by himself at the far end, and Harris kept out of his way because he was English. He feared he might be in business, possibly even in the silk business, and that he would perhaps talk on the subject. The other traveller, however, was a Catholic priest. He was a little man who ate his salad with a knife, yet so gently that it was almost inoffensive, and it was the sight of 'the cloth' that recalled his memory of the old antagonism. Harris mentioned by way of conversation the object of his sentimental journey, and the priest looked up sharply at him with raised eyebrows and an expression of surprise and suspicion that somehow piqued him. He ascribed it to his difference of belief.

'Yes,' went on the silk merchant, pleased to talk of what his mind was so full, 'and it was a curious experience for an English boy to be dropped down into a school of a hundred foreigners. I well remember the loneliness and intolerable *Heimweh* of it at first.' His German was very fluent.

The priest opposite looked up from his cold veal and potato salad and smiled. It was a nice face. He explained quietly that he did not belong here, but was making a tour of the parishes of Württemberg and Baden.

'It was a strict life,' added Harris. 'We English, I remember, used to call it *Gefängnisleben* – prison life!'

The face of the other, for some unaccountable reason, darkened. After a slight pause, and more by way of politeness than because he wished to continue the subject, he said quietly:

'It was a flourishing school in those days, of course. Afterwards, I have heard——' He shrugged his shoulders slightly, and the odd look – it almost seemed a look of alarm – came back into his eyes. The sentence remained unfinished.

Something in the tone of the man seemed to his listener uncalled for – in a sense reproachful, singular. Harris bridled in spite of himself.

'It has changed?' he asked. 'I can hardly believe——'

'You have not heard, then?' observed the priest gently, making a gesture as though to cross himself, yet not actually completing it. 'You have not heard what happened there before it was abandoned——?'

It was very childish, of course, and perhaps he was overtired and overwrought in some way, but the words and manner of the little priest seemed to him so offensive – so disproportionately offensive – that he hardly noticed the concluding sentence. He recalled the old bitterness and the old antagonism, and for a moment he almost lost his temper.

'Nonsense,' he interrupted with a forced laugh, '*Unsinn!* You must forgive me, sir, for contradicting you. But I was a pupil there myself. I was at school there. There was no place like it. I cannot believe that anything serious could have happened to – to take away its character. The devotion of the Brothers would be difficult to equal anywhere——'

He broke off suddenly, realising that his voice had been raised unduly and that the man at the far end of the table might understand German; and at the same moment he looked up and saw that this individual's eyes were fixed upon his face intently. They were peculiarly bright. Also they were rather wonderful eyes, and the way they met his own served in some way he could not understand to convey both a reproach and a warning. The whole face of the stranger, indeed, made a vivid impression upon him for it was a face, he now noticed for the first time, in whose presence one would not willingly have said or done anything unworthy. Harris could not explain to himself how it was he had not become conscious sooner of its presence.

But he could have bitten off his tongue for having so far forgotten himself. The little priest lapsed into silence. Only once he said, looking up and speaking in a low voice that was not intended to be overheard, but that evidently *was* overheard, 'You will find it different.' Presently he rose and left the table with a polite bow that included both the others, and, after him, from the far end rose also the figure in the tweed suit, leaving Harris by himself.

He sat on for a bit in the darkening room, sipping his coffee and smoking his fifteen-pfennig cigar, till the girl came in to light the oil lamps. He felt vexed with himself for his lapse from good manners, yet hardly able to account for it. Most likely, he reflected, he had been annoyed because the priest had unintentionally changed the pleasant character of his dream by introducing a jarring note. Later he must seek an opportunity to make amends. At present, however, he was too impatient for his walk to the school, and he took his stick and hat and passed out into the open air.

And, as he crossed before the Gasthaus, he noticed that the priest and the man in the tweed suit were engaged already in such deep conversation that they hardly noticed him as he passed and raised his hat.

He started off briskly, well remembering the way, and hoping to reach the village in time to have a word with one of the Brüders. They might even ask him in for a cup of coffee. He felt sure of his welcome, and the old memories were in full possession once more. The hour of return was a matter of no consequence whatever.

It was then just after seven o'clock, and the October evening was drawing in with chill airs from the recesses of the forest. The road plunged straight from the railway clearing into its depths, and in a very few minutes the trees engulfed him and the clack of his boots fell dead and echoless against the serried stems of a million firs. It was very black; one trunk was hardly distinguishable from another. He walked smartly, swinging his holly stick. Once or twice he passed a peasant on his way to bed, and the guttural 'Gruss Gott', unheard for so long, emphasised the passage of time, while yet making it seem as nothing. A fresh group of pictures crowded his mind. Again the figures of former schoolfellows flitted out of the forest and kept pace by his side, whispering of the doings of long ago. One reverie stepped hard upon the heels of another. Every turn in the road, every clearing of the forest, he knew, and each in turn brought forgotten associations to life. He enjoyed himself thoroughly.

He marched on and on. There was powdered gold in the sky till the moon rose, and then a wind of faint silver spread silently between the earth and stars. He saw the tips of the fir trees shimmer, and heard them whisper as the breeze turned their needles towards the light. The mountain air was indescribably sweet. The road shone like the foam of a river through the gloom.

White moths flitted here and there like silent thoughts across his path, and a hundred smells greeted him from the forest caverns across the years.

Then, when he least expected it, the trees fell away abruptly on both sides, and he stood on the edge of the village clearing.

He walked faster. There lay the familiar outlines of the houses, sheeted with silver; there stood the trees in the little central square with the fountain and small green lawns; there loomed the shape of the church next to the Gasthof der Brüdergemeinde; and just beyond, dimly rising into the sky, he saw with a sudden thrill the mass of the huge school building, blocked castle-like with deep shadows in the moonlight, standing square and formidable to face him after the silences of more than a quarter of a century.

He passed quickly down the deserted village street and stopped close beneath its shadow, staring up at the walls that had once held him prisoner for two years – two unbroken years of discipline and homesickness. Memories and emotions surged through his mind; for the most vivid sensations of his youth had focused about this spot, and it was here he had first begun to live and learn values. Not a single footstep broke the silence, though lights glimmered here and there through cottage windows; but when he looked up at the high walls of the school, draped now in shadow, he easily imagined that well-known faces crowded to the windows to greet him – closed windows that really reflected only moonlight and the gleam of stars.

This, then, was the old school building, standing foursquare to the world, with its shuttered windows, its lofty, tiled roof, and the spiked lightning conductors pointing like black and taloned fingers from the corners. For a long time he stood and stared. Then, presently, he came to himself again, and realised to his joy that a light still shone in the windows of the *Brüderstube*.

He turned from the road and passed through the iron railings; then climbed the twelve stone steps and stood facing the black wooden door with the heavy bars of iron, a door he had once loathed and dreaded with the hatred and passion of an imprisoned soul, but now looked upon tenderly with a sort of boyish delight.

Almost timorously he pulled the rope and listened with a tremor of excitement to the clanging of the bell deep within the building. And the long-forgotten sound brought the past before him with such a vivid sense of reality that he positively shivered. It was like the magic bell in the fairy-tale that rolls back the curtain of Time and summons the figures from the shadows of the dead. He had never felt so sentimental in his life. It was like being young again. And, at the same time, he began to bulk rather large in his own eyes with a certain spurious importance. He was a big man from the world of strife and action. In this little place of peaceful dreams would he, perhaps, not cut something of a figure?

'I'll try once more,' he thought after a long pause, seizing the iron bell-rope, and was just about to pull it when a step sounded on the stone passage within, and the huge door slowly swung open.

A tall man with a rather severe cast of countenance stood facing him in silence.

'I must apologise – it is somewhat late,' he began a trifle pompously, 'but the fact is I am an old pupil. I have only just arrived and really could not restrain myself.' His German seemed not quite so fluent as usual. 'My interest is so great. I was here in 'seventy.'

The other opened the door wider and at once bowed him in with a smile of genuine welcome.

'I am Brüder Kalkmann,' he said quietly in a deep voice. 'I myself was a master here about that time. It is a great pleasure always to welcome a former pupil.' He looked at him very keenly for a few seconds, and then added, 'I think, too, it is splendid of you to come – very splendid.'

'It is a very great pleasure,' Harris replied, delighted with his reception.

The dimly-lighted corridor with its flooring of grey stone, and the familiar sound of a German voice echoing through it – with the peculiar intonation the Brothers always used in speaking – all combined to lift him bodily, as it were, into the dream-atmosphere of long-forgotten days. He stepped gladly into the building and the door shut with the familiar thunder that completed the reconstruction of the past. He almost felt the old sense of imprisonment, of aching nostalgia, of having lost his liberty.

Harris sighed involuntarily and turned towards his host, who returned his smile faintly and then led the way down the corridor.

'The boys have retired,' he explained, 'and, as you remember, we keep early hours here. But, at least, you will join us for a little while in the *Brüderstube* and enjoy a cup of coffee.' This was precisely what the silk merchant had hoped, and he accepted with an alacrity that he intended to be tempered by graciousness. 'And tomorrow,' continued the Brüder, 'you must come and spend a whole day with us. You may even find acquaintances, for several pupils of your day have come back here as masters.'

For one brief second there passed into the man's eyes a look that made the visitor start. But it vanished as quickly as it came. It was impossible to define. Harris convinced himself it was the effect of a shadow cast by the lamp they had just passed on the wall. He dismissed it from his mind.

'You are very kind, I'm sure,' he said politely. 'It is perhaps a greater pleasure to me than you can imagine to see the place again. Ah' – he stopped short opposite a door with the upper half of glass and peered in – 'surely there is one of the music rooms where I used to practise the violin. How it comes back to me after all these years!'

Brüder Kalkmann stopped indulgently, smiling, to allow his guest a moment's inspection.

'You still have the boys' orchestra? I remember I used to play *"zweite Geige"* in it. Brüder Schliemann conducted at the piano. Dear me, I can see him now with his long black hair and – and ——' He stopped abruptly. Again the odd, dark look passed over the stern face of his companion. For an instant it seemed curiously familiar.

'We still keep up the pupils' orchestra,' he said, 'but Brüder Schliemann, I am sorry to say——' he hesitated an instant, and then added, 'Brüder Schliemann is dead.'

'Indeed, indeed,' said Harris quickly. 'I am sorry to hear it.' He was conscious of a faint feeling of distress, but whether it arose from the news of his old music teacher's death – or from something else – he could not quite determine. He gazed down the corridor that lost itself among shadows. In the street and village everything had seemed so much smaller than he remembered, but here, inside the school building, everything seemed so much bigger. The corridor was loftier and longer, more spacious and vast, than the mental picture he had preserved. His thoughts wandered dreamily for an instant.

He glanced up and saw the face of the Brüder watching him with a smile of patient indulgence.

'Your memories possess you,' he observed gently, and the stern look passed into something almost pitying.

'You are right,' returned the man of silk, 'they do. This was the most wonderful period of my whole life in a sense. At the time I hated it——' He hesitated, not wishing to hurt the Brother's feelings.

'According to English ideas it seemed strict, of course,' the other said persuasively, so that he went on.

'——Yes, partly that; and partly the ceaseless nostalgia, and the solitude which came from never being really alone. In English schools the boys enjoy peculiar freedom, you know.'

Brüder Kalkmann, he saw, was listening intently.

'But it produced one result that I have never wholly lost,' he continued self-consciously, 'and am grateful for.'

'*Ach! Wie so, denn!*'

'The constant inner pain threw me headlong into your religious life, so that the whole force of my being seemed to project itself towards the search for a deeper satisfaction – a real resting-place for the soul. During my two years here I yearned for God in my boyish way as perhaps I have never yearned for anything since. Moreover, I have never quite lost that sense of peace and inward joy which accompanied the search. I can never quite forget this school and the deep things it taught me.'

He paused at the end of his long speech, and a brief silence fell between them. He feared he had said too much, or expressed himself clumsily in the foreign language, and when Brüder Kalkmann laid a hand upon his shoulder, he gave a little involuntary start.

'So that my memories perhaps do possess me rather strongly,' he added apologetically; 'and this long corridor, these rooms, that barred and gloomy front door, all touch chords that – that——' His German failed him and he glanced at his companion with an explanatory smile and gesture. But the Brother had removed his hand from his shoulder and was standing with his back to him, looking down the passage.

'Naturally, naturally so,' he said hastily without turning round. '*Es ist doch selbstverständlich.* We shall all understand.'

Then he turned suddenly, and Harris saw that his face had turned most oddly and disagreeably sinister. It may only have been the shadows again playing their tricks with the wretched oil lamps on the wall, for the dark expression passed instantly as they retraced their steps down the corridor, but the Englishman somehow got the impression that he had said something to give offence, something that was not quite to the other's taste. Opposite the door of the *Brüderstube* they stopped. Harris realised that it was late and he had possibly stayed talking too long. He made a tentative effort to leave, but his companion would not hear of it.

'You must have a cup of coffee with us,' he said firmly as though he meant it, 'and my colleagues will be delighted to see you. Some of them will remember you, perhaps.'

The sound of voices came pleasantly through the door, men's voices talking together. Brüder Kalkmann turned the handle and they entered a room ablaze with light and full of people.

'Ah – but your name?' he whispered, bending down to catch the reply; 'you have not told me your name yet.'

'Harris,' said the Englishman quickly as they went in. He felt nervous as he crossed the threshold, but ascribed the momentary trepidation to the fact that he was breaking the strictest rule of the whole establishment, which forbade a boy under severest penalties to come near this holy of holies where the masters took their brief leisure.

'Ah, yes, of course – Harris,' repeated the other as though he remembered it. 'Come in, Herr Harris, come in, please. Your visit will be immensely appreciated. It is really very fine, very wonderful of you to have come in this way.'

The door closed behind them and, in the sudden light which made his sight swim for a moment, the exaggeration of the language escaped his attention. He heard the voice of Brüder Kalkmann introducing him. He spoke very loud, indeed, unnecessarily – absurdly loud, Harris thought.

'Brothers,' he announced, 'it is my pleasure and privilege to introduce to you Herr Harris from England. He has just arrived to make us a little visit, and I have already expressed to him on behalf of us all the satisfaction we feel that he is here. He was, as you remember, a pupil in the year 'seventy.'

It was very formal, a very German introduction, but Harris rather liked it. It made him feel important and he appreciated the tact that made it almost seem as though he had been expected.

The black forms rose and bowed; Harris bowed; Kalkmann bowed. Everyone was very polite and very courtly. The room swam with moving figures; the light dazzled him after the gloom of the corridor; there was thick cigar smoke in the atmosphere. He took the chair that was offered to him between two of the Brothers, and sat down, feeling vaguely that his perceptions were not quite as keen and accurate as usual. He felt a trifle dazed perhaps, and the spell of the past came strongly over him, confusing the immediate present and making everything dwindle oddly to the dimensions of long ago. He seemed to pass under the mastery of a great mood that was a composite reproduction of all the moods of his forgotten boyhood.

Then he pulled himself together with a sharp effort and entered into the conversation that had begun again to buzz round him. Moreover, he entered into it with keen pleasure, for the Brothers – there were perhaps a dozen of them in the little room – treated him with a charm of manner that speedily made him feel one of themselves. This, again, was a very subtle delight to him. He felt that he had stepped out of the greedy, vulgar, self-seeking world, the world of silk and markets and profit-making – stepped into the cleaner atmosphere where spiritual ideals were paramount and life was simple and devoted. It all charmed him inexpressibly, so that he realised – yes, in a sense – the degradation of his twenty years' absorption in business. This keen atmosphere under the stars where men thought only of their souls, and of the souls of others, was too rarefied for the world he was now associated with. He found himself making comparisons to his own disadvantage – comparisons with the mystical little dreamer that had stepped thirty years before from the stern peace of this devout community, and the man of the world that he had since become – and the contrast made him shiver with a keen regret and something like self-contempt.

He glanced round at the other faces floating towards him

through tobacco smoke – this acrid cigar smoke he remembered so well: how keen they were, how strong, placid, touched with the nobility of great aims and unselfish purposes. At one or two he looked particularly. He hardly knew why. They rather fascinated him. There was something so very stern and un-compromising about them, and something, too, oddly, subtly, familiar, that yet just eluded him. But whenever their eyes met his own they held undeniable welcome in them; and some held more – a kind of perplexed admiration, he thought, something that was between esteem and deference. This note of respect in all the faces was very flattering to his vanity.

Coffee was served presently, made by a black-haired Brother who sat in the corner by the piano and bore a marked resem-blance to Brüder Schliemann, the musical director of thirty years ago. Harris exchanged bows with him when he took the cup from his white hands, which he noticed were like the hands of a woman. He lit a cigar, offered to him by his neighbour, with whom he was chatting delightfully, and who, in the glare of the lighted match, reminded him sharply for a moment of Brüder Pagel, his former room-master.

'*Es ist wirklich merkwürdig,*' he said, 'how many resemblances I see, or imagine. It is really *very* curious!'

'Yes,' replied the other, peering at him over his coffee cup, 'the spell of the place is wonderfully strong. I can well under-stand that the old faces rise before your mind's eye – almost to the exclusion of ourselves perhaps.'

They both laughed pleasantly. It was soothing to find his mood understood and appreciated. And they passed on to talk of the mountain village, its isolation, its remoteness from the worldly life, its peculiar fitness for meditation and worship, and for spiritual development – of a certain kind.

'And your coming back in this way, Herr Harris, has pleased us all so much,' joined in the Brother on his left. 'We esteem you for it most highly. We honour you for it.'

Harris made a deprecating gesture. 'I fear, for my part, it is only a very selfish pleasure,' he said a trifle unctuously.

'Not all would have had the courage,' added the one who resembled Brüder Pagel.

'You mean,' said Harris, a little puzzled, 'the disturbing memories——?'

Brüder Pagel looked at him steadily, with unmistakable admiration and respect. 'I mean that most men hold so strongly to life, and can give up so little for their beliefs,' he said gravely.

The Englishman felt slightly uncomfortable. These worthy men really made too much of his sentimental journey. Besides, the talk was getting a little out of his depth. He hardly followed it.

'The worldly life still has *some* charms for me,' he replied smilingly, as though to indicate that sainthood was not yet quite within his grasp.

'All the more, then, must we honour you for so freely coming,' said the Brother on his left; 'so unconditionally!'

A pause followed, and the silk merchant felt relieved when the conversation took a more general turn, although he noted that it never travelled very far from the subject of his visit and the wonderful situation of the lonely village for the men who wished to develop their spiritual powers and practise the rites of a high worship. Others joined in, complimenting him on his knowledge of the language, making him feel utterly at his ease, yet at the same time a little uncomfortable by the excess of their admiration. After all, it was such a very small thing to do, this sentimental journey.

The time passed along quickly; the coffee was excellent, the cigars soft and of the nutty flavour he loved. At length, fearing to outstay his welcome, he rose reluctantly to take his leave. But the others would not hear of it. It was not often a former pupil returned to visit them in this simple, unaffected way. The night was young. If necessary they could even find him a corner in the great *Schlafzimmer* upstairs. He was easily persuaded to stay a little longer. Somehow he had become the centre of the little party. He felt pleased, flattered, honoured.

'And perhaps Brüder Schliemann will play something for us – now.'

It was Kalkmann speaking, and Harris started visibly as he heard the name, and saw the black-haired man by the piano turn with a smile. For Schliemann was the name of his old music director, who was dead. Could this be his son? They were so exactly alike.

'If Brüder Meyer has not put his Amati to bed, I will accompany him,' said the musician suggestively, looking across at a man whom Harris had not yet noticed, and who, he now saw, was the very image of a former master of that name.

Meyer rose and excused himself with a little bow, and the Englishman quickly observed that he had a peculiar gesture as though his neck had a false join on to the body just below the collar and feared it might break. Meyer of old had this trick of movement. He remembered how the boys used to copy it.

He glanced sharply from face to face, feeling as though some silent, unseen process were changing everything about him. All the faces seemed oddly familiar. Pagel, the Brother he had been talking with, was of course the image of Pagel, his former room-master; and Kalkmann, he now realised for the first time, was the very twin of another master whose name he had quite forgotten, but whom he used to dislike intensely in the old days. And, through the smoke, peering at him from the corners of the room, he saw that all the Brothers about him had the faces he had known and lived with long ago – Rost, Fluheim, Meinert, Rigel, Gysin.

He stared hard, suddenly grown more alert, and everywhere saw, or fancied he saw, strange likenesses, ghostly resemblances – more, the identical faces of years ago. There was something queer about it all, something not quite right, something that made him feel uneasy. He shook himself, mentally and actually, blowing the smoke from before his eyes with a long breath, and as he did so he noticed to his dismay that everyone was fixedly staring. They were watching him.

This brought him to his senses. As an Englishman, and a foreigner, he did not wish to be rude, or to do anything to make himself foolishly conspicuous and spoil the harmony of the evening. He was a guest, and a privileged guest at that. Besides, the music had already begun. Brüder Schliemann's long white fingers were caressing the keys to some purpose.

He subsided into his chair and smoked with half-closed eyes that yet saw everything.

But the shudder had established itself in his being, and, whether he would or not, it kept repeating itself. As a town, far up some inland river, feels the pressure of the distant sea, so he became aware that the mighty forces from somewhere beyond his ken were urging themselves up against his soul in this smoky little room. He began to feel exceedingly ill at ease.

And as the music filled the air his mind began to clear. Like a lifted veil there rose up something that had hitherto obscured his vision. The words of the priest at the railway inn flashed across his brain unbidden: 'You will find it different.' And also, though why he could not tell, he saw mentally the strong, rather wonderful eyes of that other guest at the supper table, the man who had overheard his conversation, and had later got into earnest talk with the priest. He took out his watch and stole a glance at it. Two hours had slipped by. It was already eleven o'clock.

Schliemann, meanwhile, utterly absorbed in his music, was playing a solemn measure. The piano sang marvellously. The power of a great conviction, the simplicity of great art, the vital spiritual message of a soul that had found itself – all this, and more, were in the chords, and yet somehow the music was what can only be described as impure – atrociously and diabolically

impure. And the piece itself, although Harris did not re-
cognise it as anything familiar, was surely the music of a
Mass – huge, majestic, sombre? It stalked through the smoky
room with slow power, like the passage of something that was
mighty, yet profoundly intimate, and as it went there stirred
into each and every face about him the signature of the enor-
mous forces of which it was the audible symbol. The countenances round him turned sinister, but not idly, negatively sinister:
they grew dark with purpose. He suddenly recalled the face of
Brüder Kalkmann in the corridor earlier in the evening. The
motives of their secret souls rose to the eyes, and mouths, and
foreheads, and hung there for all to see like the black banners of
an assembly of ill-starred and fallen creatures. Demons – was
the horrible word that flashed through his brain like a sheet of
fire.

When this sudden discovery leaped out upon him, for a
moment he lost his self-control. Without waiting to think and
weigh his extraordinary impression, he did a very foolish but a
very natural thing. Feeling himself irresistibly driven by the
sudden stress to some kind of action, he sprang to his feet – and
screamed! To his own utter amazement he stood up and
shrieked aloud!

But no one stirred. No one, apparently, took the slightest
notice of his absurdly wild behaviour. It was almost as if no one
but himself had heard the scream at all – as though the music
had drowned it and swallowed it up – as though after all perhaps
he had not really screamed as loudly as he imagined, or had not
screamed at all.

Then, as he glanced at the motionless, dark faces before him,
something of utter cold passed into his being, touching his very
soul. . . . All emotion cooled suddenly, leaving him like a
receding tide. He sat down again, ashamed, mortified, angry
with himself for behaving like a fool and a boy. And the music,
meanwhile, continued to issue from the white and snake-like

fingers of Brüder Schliemann, as poisoned wine might issue from the weirdly-fashioned necks of antique phials.

And, with the rest of them, Harris drank it in.

Forcing himself to believe that he had been the victim of some kind of illusory perception, he vigorously restrained his feelings. Then the music presently ceased, and every one applauded and began to talk at once, laughing, changing seats, complimenting the player and behaving naturally and easily as though nothing out of the way had happened. The faces appeared normal once more. The Brothers crowded round their visitor, and he joined in their talk and even heard himself thanking the gifted musician.

But, at the same time, he found himself edging towards the door, nearer and nearer, changing his chair when possible, and joining the groups that stood closest to the way of escape.

'I must thank you all *tausendmal* for my little reception and the great pleasure – the very great honour you have done me,' he began in decided tones at length, 'but I fear I have trespassed far too long already on your hospitality. Moreover, I have some distance to walk to my inn.'

A chorus of voices greeted his words. They would not hear of his going – at least not without first partaking of refreshment. They produced pumpernickel from one cupboard, and rye-bread and sausage from another, and all began to talk again and eat. More coffee was made, fresh cigars lighted, and Brüder Meyer took out his violin and began to tune it softly.

'There is always a bed upstairs if Herr Harris will accept it,' said one.

'And it is difficult to find the way out now, for all the doors are locked,' laughed another loudly.

'Let us take our simple pleasures as they come,' cried a third. 'Brüder Harris will understand how we appreciate the honour of this last visit of his.'

They made a dozen excuses. They all laughed, as though the

politeness of their words was but formal, and veiled thinly – more and more thinly – a very different meaning.

'And the hour of midnight draws near,' added Brüder Kalkmann with a charming smile, but in a voice that sounded to the Englishman like the grating of iron hinges.

Their German seemed to him more and more difficult to understand. He noted that they called him 'Brüder' too, classing him as one of themselves.

And then suddenly he had a flash of keener perception, and realised with a creeping of his flesh that he had all along misinterpreted – grossly misinterpreted – all they had been saying. They had talked about the beauty of the place, its isolation and remoteness from the world, its peculiar fitness for certain kinds of spiritual development and worship – yet hardly, he now grasped, in the sense in which he had taken the words. They had meant something different. Their spiritual powers, their desire for loneliness, their passion for worship, were not the powers, the solitude, or the worship that *he* meant and understood. He was playing the part in some horrible masquerade; he was among men who cloaked their lives with religion in order to follow their real purposes unseen of men.

What did it all mean? How had he blundered into so equivocal a situation? Had he blundered into it at all? Had he not rather been led into it, deliberately led? His thoughts grew dreadfully confused, and his confidence in himself began to fade. And why, he suddenly thought again, were they so impressed by the mere fact of his coming to revisit his old school? What was it they so admired and wondered at in his simple act? Why did they set such store upon his having the courage to come, to 'give himself so freely', 'unconditionally' as one of them had expressed it with such a mockery of exaggeration?

Fear stirred in his heart most horribly, and he found no answer to any of his questionings. Only one thing he now understood quite clearly: it was their purpose to keep him here. They did not intend that he should go. And from this moment he realised that they were sinister, formidable and, in some way he had yet to discover, inimical to himself, inimical to his life. And the phrase one of them had used a moment ago — 'this *last* visit of his' — rose before his eyes in letters of flame.

Harris was not a man of action, and had never known in all the course of his career what it meant to be in a situation of real danger. He was not necessarily a coward, though, perhaps, a man of untried nerve. He realised at last plainly that he was in a very awkward predicament indeed, and that he had to deal with men who were utterly in earnest. What their intentions were he only vaguely guessed. His mind, indeed, was too confused for definite ratiocination, and he was only able to follow blindly the strongest instincts that moved in him. It never occurred to him that the Brothers might all be mad, or that he himself might have temporarily lost his senses and be suffering under some terrible delusion. In fact, nothing occurred to him — he realised nothing except that he meant to escape — and the quicker the better. A tremendous revulsion of feeling set in and overpowered him.

Accordingly, without further protest for the moment, he ate his pumpernickel and drank his coffee, talking meanwhile as naturally and pleasantly as he could, and when a suitable interval had passed, he rose to his feet and announced once more that he must now take his leave. He spoke very quietly, but very decidedly. No one hearing him could doubt that he meant what he said. He had got very close to the door by this time.

'I regret,' he said, using his best German, and speaking to a hushed room, 'that our pleasant evening must come to an end, but it is now time for me to wish you all good-night.' And then, as no one said anything, he added, though with a trifle less assurance, 'And I thank you all most sincerely for your hospitality.'

'On the contrary,' replied Kalkmann instantly, rising from his chair and ignoring the hand the Englishman had stretched out to him, 'it is we who have to thank you; and we do so most gratefully and sincerely.'

And at the same moment at least half a dozen of the Brothers took up their position between himself and the door.

'You are very good to say so,' Harris replied as firmly as he could manage, noticing this movement out of the corner of his eye, 'but really I had no conception that – my little chance visit could have afforded you so much pleasure.' He moved another step nearer the door, but Brüder Schliemann came across the room quickly and stood in front of him. His attitude was uncompromising. A dark and terrible expression had come into his face.

'But it was *not* by chance that you came, Brüder Harris,' he said so that all the room could hear; 'surely we have not misunderstood your presence here?' He raised his black eyebrows.

'No, no,' the Englishman hastened to reply. 'I was – I am delighted to be here. I told you what pleasure it gave me to find myself among you. Do not misunderstand me, I beg.' His voice faltered a little, and he had difficulty in finding the words. More and more, too, he had difficulty in understanding *their* words.

'Of course,' interposed Brüder Kalkmann in his iron bass, '*we* have not misunderstood. You have come back in the spirit of true and unselfish devotion. You offer yourself freely, and we all appreciate it. It is your willingness and nobility that have so completely won our veneration and respect.' A faint murmur of applause ran round the room. 'What we all delight in – what our great Master will especially delight in – is the value of your spontaneous and voluntary——'

He used a word Harris did not understand. He said *'Opfer'*. The bewildered Englishman searched his brain for the translation, and searched in vain, for the life of him he could not remember what it meant. But the word, for all his inability to translate it, touched his soul with ice. It was worse, far worse, than anything he had imagined. He felt like a lost, helpless

30

creature, and all power to fight sank out of him from that mom-
ment.

'It is magnificent to be such a willing——' added Schliemann,
sidling up to him with a dreadful leer on his face. He made use
of the same word – '*Opfer*'

God! What could it all mean? 'Offer himself'! 'True spirit of
devotion'! 'Willing', 'unselfish', 'magnificent'! *Opfer, Opfer,
Opfer!* What in the name of heaven did it mean, that strange,
mysterious word that struck such terror into his heart?

He made a valiant effort to keep his presence of mind and hold
his nerves steady. Turning, he saw that Kalkmann's face was a
dead white. Kalkmann! He understood that well enough.
Kalkmann meant 'Man of Chalk'; he knew that. But what did
'*Opfer*' mean? That was the real key to the situation. Words
poured through his disordered mind in an endless stream –
unusual, rare words he had perhaps heard but once in his life –
while '*Opfer*', a word in common use, entirely escaped him.
What an extraordinary mockery it all was!

Then Kalkmann, pale as death, but his face hard as iron, spoke
a few low words that he did not catch, and the Brothers standing
by the walls at once turned the lamps down so that the room
became dim. In the half light he could only just discern their
faces and movements.

'It is time,' he heard Kalkmann's remorseless voice continue
just behind him. 'The hour of midnight is at hand. Let us
prepare. He comes! He comes; Brüder Asmodelius comes!' His
voice rose to a chant.

And the sound of that name, for some extraordinary reason,
was terrible – utterly terrible; so that Harris shook from head to
foot as he heard it. Its utterance filled the air like soft thunder,
and a hush came over the whole room. Forces rose all about him,
transforming the normal into the horrible, and the spirit of
craven fear ran through all his being, bringing him to the
verge of collapse.

Asmodelius! Asmodelius! The name was appalling. For he understood at last to whom it referred and the meaning that lay between its great syllables. At the same instant, too, he suddenly understood the meaning of that unremembered word. The import of the word *'Opfer'* flashed upon his soul like a message of death.

He thought of making a wild effort to reach the door, but the weakness of his trembling knees, and the row of black figures that stood between, dissuaded him at once. He would have screamed for help, but remembering the emptiness of the vast building, and the loneliness of the situation, he understood that no help could come that way, and he kept his lips closed. He stood still and did nothing. But he knew now what was coming.

Two of the brothers approached and took him gently by the arm.

'Brüder Asmodelius accepts you,' they whispered; 'are you ready?'

Then he found his tongue and tried to speak. 'But what have I to do with this Brüder Asm – Asmo——?' he stammered, a desperate rush of words crowding vainly behind the halting tongue.

The name refused to pass his lips. He could not pronounce it as they did. He could not pronounce it at all. His sense of help-lessness then entered the acute stage, for this inability to speak the name produced a fresh sense of quite horrible confusion in his mind, and he became extraordinarily agitated.

'I came here for a friendly visit,' he tried to say with a great effort, but, to his intense dismay, he heard his voice saying something quite different, and actually making use of that very word they had all used: 'I came here as a willing *Opfer*,' he heard his own voice say, *'and I am quite ready.'*

He was lost beyond all recall now! Not alone his mind, but the very muscles of his body had passed out of control. He felt that he was hovering on the confines of a phantom or demon-world –

a world in which the name they had spoken constituted the Master-name, the word of ultimate power.

What followed he heard and saw as in a nightmare!

'In the half light that veils all truth, let us prepare to worship and adore,' chanted Schliemann, who had preceded him to the end of the room.

'In the mists that protect our faces before the Black Throne, let us make ready the willing victim,' echoed Kalkmann in his great bass.

They raised their faces, listening expectantly, as a roaring sound, like the passing of mighty projectiles, filled the air, far, far away, very wonderful, very forbidding. The walls of the room trembled.

'He comes! He comes! He comes!' chanted the Brothers in chorus.

The sound of roaring died away, and an atmosphere of still and utter cold established itself over all. Then Kalkmann, dark and unutterably stern, turned in the dim light and faced the rest.

'Asmodelius, our *Haupbrüder*, is about us,' he cried in a voice that even while it shook was yet a voice of iron; 'Asmodelius is about us. Make ready.'

There followed a pause in which no one stirred or spoke. A tall Brother approached the Englishman; but Kalkmann held up his hand.

'Let the eyes remain uncovered,' he said, 'in honour of so freely giving himself.' And to his horror Harris then realised for the first time that his hands were already fastened to his sides.

The Brother retreated again silently, and in the pause that followed all the figures about him dropped to their knees, leaving him standing alone, and as they dropped, in voices hushed with mingled reverence and awe, they cried softly, odiously, appallingly the name of the Being whom they momentarily expected to appear.

Then, at the end of the room, where the windows seemed to

have disappeared so that he saw the stars, there rose into view far up against the night sky, grand and terrible, the outline of a man. A kind of grey glory enveloped it so that it resembled a steel-cased statue, immense, imposing, horrific in its distant splendour; while, at the same time, the face was so spiritually mighty, yet so proudly, so austerely sad, that Harris felt as he stared, that the sight was more than his eyes could meet, and that in another moment the power of vision would fail him altogether, and he must sink into utter nothingness.

So remote and inaccessible hung this figure that it was impossible to gauge anything as to its size, yet at the same time so strangely close, that when the grey radiance from its mightily broken visage, august and mournful, beat down upon his soul, pulsing like some dark star with the powers of spiritual evil, he felt almost as though he were looking into a face no farther removed from him in space than the face of any one of the Brothers who stood by his side.

And then the room filled and trembled with sounds that Harris understood full well were the failing voices of others who had preceded him in a long series down the years. There came first a plain, sharp cry, as of a man in the last anguish, choking for his breath, and yet, with the very final expiration of it, breathing the name of the Worship -- of the dark Being who rejoiced to hear it. The cries of the strangled; the short, running gasp of the suffocated; and the smothered gurgling of the tightened throat, all these, and more, echoed back and forth between the walls, the very walls in which he now stood a prisoner, a sacrificial victim. The cries, too, not alone of the broken bodies, but -- far worse -- of beaten, broken souls. And as the ghastly chorus rose and fell, there came also the faces of the lost and unhappy creatures to whom they belonged, and, against that curtain of pale grey light, he saw float past him in the air, an array of white and piteous human countenances that seemed to beckon and gibber at him as though he were already one of themselves.

Slowly, too, as the voices rose, and the pallid crew sailed past, that giant form of grey descended from the sky and approached the room that contained the worshippers and their prisoner. Hands rose and sank about them in the darkness, and he felt that he was being draped in other garments than his own; a circlet of ice seemed to run about his head, while round the waist, enclosing the fastened arms, he felt a girdle tightly drawn. At last, about his very throat, there ran a soft and silken touch which, better than if there had been full light, and a mirror held to his face, he understood to be the cord of sacrifice – and of death.

At this moment the Brothers, still prostrate upon the floor, began again their mournful, yet impassioned chanting, and as they did so a strange thing happened. For, apparently without moving or altering its position, the huge Figure seemed, at once and suddenly, to be inside the room, almost beside him, and to fill the space around him to the exclusion of all else.

He was now beyond all ordinary sensations of fear, only a drab feeling as of death – the death of the soul – stirred in his heart. His thoughts no longer even beat vainly for space. The end was near, and he knew it.

The dreadfully chanting voices rose about him in a wave: 'We worship! We adore! We offer!' The sounds filled his ears and hammered, almost meaningless, upon his brain.

Then the majestic grey face turned slowly downwards upon him, and his very soul passed outwards and seemed to become absorbed in the sea of those anguished eyes. At the same moment a dozen hands forced him to his knees, and in the air before him he saw the arm of Kalkmann upraised, and felt the pressure about his throat grow strong.

It was in this awful moment, when he had given up all hope, and the help of gods or men seemed beyond question, that a strange thing happened. For before his fading and terrified vision, there slid, as in a dream of light – yet without apparent rhyme or reason – wholly unbidden and unexplained – the face of that other man at the supper table of the railway inn. And the sight, even mentally, of that strong, wholesome, vigorous English face, inspired him suddenly with a new courage.

It was but a flash of fading vision before he sank into a dark and terrible death, yet, in some inexplicable way, the sight of that face stirred in him unconquerable hope and the certainty of deliverance. It was a face of power, a face, he now realised, of simple goodness such as might have been seen by men of old on the shores of Galilee; a face, by heaven, that could conquer even the devils of outer space.

And, in his despair and abandonment, he called upon it, and called with no uncertain accents. He found his voice in this overwhelming moment to some purpose; though the words he actually used, and whether they were in German or English, he could never remember. Their effect, nevertheless, was instantaneous. The Brothers understood, and that grey Figure of evil understood.

For a second the confusion was terrific. There came a great shattering sound. It seemed that the very earth trembled. But all Harris remembered afterwards was that voices rose about him in the clamour of terrified alarm –

'A man of power is among us! A man of God!'

The vast sound was repeated – the rushing through space as of huge projectiles – and he sank to the floor of the room, unconscious. The entire scene had vanished, vanished like smoke over the roof of a cottage when the wind blows.

And, by his side, sat down a slight un-German figure – the figure of the stranger at the inn – the man who had the 'rather wonderful eyes'.

When Harris came to himself he felt cold. He was lying under the open sky, and the cool air of field and forest was blowing upon his face. He sat up and looked about him. The memory of the late scene was still horribly in his mind, but no vestige of it remained. No walls or ceiling enclosed him; he was no longer in a room at all. There were no lamps turned low, no cigar smoke, no black forms of sinister worshippers, no tremendous grey Figure hovering beyond the windows.

Open space was about him, and he was lying on a pile of bricks and mortar, his clothes soaked with dew, and the kind stars shining brightly overhead. He was lying, bruised and shaken, among the heaped-up debris of a ruined building.

He stood up and stared about him. There, in the shadowy distance, lay the surrounding forest, and here, close at hand, stood the outline of the village buildings. But, underfoot, beyond question, lay nothing but the broken heaps of stones that betokened a building long since crumbled to dust. Then he saw that the stones were blackened, and that great wooden beams, half burnt, half rotten, made lines through the general debris. He stood, then, among the ruins of a burnt and shattered building, the weeds and nettles proving conclusively that it had lain thus for many years.

The moon had already set behind the encircling forest, but the stars that spangled the heavens threw enough light to enable him to make quite sure of what he saw. Harris, the silk merchant, stood among these broken and burnt stones and shivered.

Then he suddenly became aware that out of the gloom a figure had risen and stood beside him. Peering at him, he thought he recognised the face of the stranger at the railway inn.

'Are *you* real?' he asked in a voice he hardly recognised as his own.

'More than real – I'm friendly,' replied the stranger; 'I followed you up here from the inn.'

Harris stood and stared for several minutes without adding anything. His teeth chattered. The least sound made him start: but the simple words in his own language, and the tone in which they were uttered, comforted him inconceivably.

'You're English too, thank God,' he said inconsequently. 'These German devils——' He broke off and put a hand to his eyes. 'But what's become of them all – and the room – and – and——' The hand travelled down to his throat and moved nervously round his neck. He drew a long, long breath of relief. 'Did I dream everything – everything?' he said distractedly.

He stared wildly about him, and the stranger moved forward and took his arm. 'Come,' he said soothingly, yet with a trace of command in the voice, 'we will move away from here. The high road or even the woods will be more to your taste, for we are standing now on one of the most haunted – and most terribly haunted – spots of the whole world.'

He guided his companion's stumbling footsteps over the broken masonry until they reached the path, the nettles stinging their hands, and Harris feeling his way like a man in a dream. Passing through the twisted iron railing they reached the path, and thence made their way to the road, shining white in the night. Once safely out of the ruins, Harris collected himself and turned to look back.

'But, how is it possible?' he exclaimed, his voice still shaking. 'How can it be possible? When I came in here I saw the building in the moonlight. They opened the door. I saw the figures and heard the voices and touched, yes touched, their very hands, and saw their damned black faces, saw them far more plainly than I see you now.' He was deeply bewildered. The glamour was still upon his eyes with a degree of reality stronger than the reality even of normal life. 'Was I so utterly deluded?'

Then suddenly the words of the stranger, which he had only half heard or understood, returned to him.

'Haunted?' he asked, looking hard at him; 'haunted, did you say?' He paused in the roadway and stared into the darkness where the building of the old school had first appeared to him. But the stranger hurried him forward.

'We shall talk more safely farther on,' he said. 'I followed you from the inn the moment I realised where you had gone. When I found you it was eleven o'clock——'

'Eleven o'clock,' said Harris, remembering with a shudder.

'——I saw you drop. I watched over you till you recovered consciousness of your own accord, and now – now I am here to guide you safely back to the inn. I have broken the spell – the glamour——'

'I owe you a great deal, sir,' interrupted Harris again, beginning to understand something of the stranger's kindness, 'but I don't understand it at all. I feel dazed and shaken.' His teeth still chattered, and spells of violent shivering passed over him from head to foot. He found that he was clinging to the other's arm. In this way they passed beyond the deserted and crumbling village and gained the high road that led homewards through the forest.

'That school building has long been in ruins,' said the man at his side presently; 'it was burnt down by order of the Elders of the community at least ten years ago. The village has been un-inhabited ever since. But the simulacra of certain ghastly events that took place under that roof in past days still continue. And the "shells" of the chief participants still enact there the dreadful deeds that led to its final destruction, and to the desertion of the whole settlement. They were devil-worshippers!'

Harris listened with beads of perspiration on his forehead that did not come alone from their leisurely pace through the cool night. Although he had seen this man but once before in his life, and had never before exchanged so much as a word with him, he felt a degree of confidence and a subtle sense of safety and well-being in his presence that were the most healing influences he could possibly have wished after the experience he had been through. For all that, he still felt as if he were walking in a dream; and though he heard every word that fell from his companion's lips, it was only the next day that the full import of all he said became fully clear to him. The presence of this quiet stranger, the man with the wonderful eyes which he felt now, rather than saw, applied a soothing anodyne to his shattered spirit that healed him through and through. And this healing influence, distilled from the dark figure at his side, satisfied his first imperative need, so that he almost forgot to realise how strange and opportune it was that the man should be there at all.

It somehow never occurred to him to ask his name, or to feel any undue wonder that one passing tourist should take so much trouble on behalf of another. He just walked by his side, listening to his quiet words, and allowing himself to enjoy the very wonderful experience after his recent ordeal, of being helped, strengthened, blessed. Only once, remembering vaguely something of his reading of years ago, he turned to the man beside him, after some more than usually remarkable words, and heard himself, almost involuntarily it seemed, putting the question: 'Then are you a Rosicrucian, sir, perhaps?' But the stranger had ignored the words, or possibly not heard them, for he continued with his talk as though unconscious of any interruption, and Harris became aware that another somewhat unusual picture had taken possession of his mind, as they walked there side by side through the cool reaches of the forest, and that he had found his imagination suddenly charged with the childhood memory of Jacob wrestling with an angel – wrestling all night with a being of superior quality whose strength eventually became his own.

'It was your abrupt conversation with the priest at supper that first put me upon the track of this remarkable occurrence,' he heard the man's quiet voice beside him in the darkness, 'and it was from him I learned after you left the story of the devil-worship that became secretly established in the heart of this simple and devout little community.'

'Devil-worship! Here——!' Harris stammered, aghast.

'Yes – here – conducted secretly for years by a group of Brothers before unexplained disappearances in the neighbourhood led to its discovery. For where could they have found a safer place in the whole wide world for their ghastly traffic and perverted powers than here, in the very precincts – under cover of the very shadow of saintliness and holy living?'

'Awful, awful!' whispered the silk merchant, 'and when I tell you the words they used to me——'

'I know it all,' the stranger said quietly. 'I saw and heard everything. My plan first was to wait till the end and then to take steps for their destruction, but in the interest of your personal safety' – he spoke with the utmost gravity and conviction – 'in the interest of the safety of your soul, I made my presence known when I did, and before the conclusion had been reached——'

'My safety! The danger, then, was real. They were alive and——' Words failed him. He stopped in the road and turned towards his companion, the shining of whose eyes he could just make out in the gloom.

'It was a concourse of the shells of violent men, spiritually-developed but evil men, seeking after death – the death of the body – to prolong their vile and unnatural existence. And had they accomplished their object you, in turn, at the death of your body, would have passed into their power and helped to swell their dreadful purposes.'

Harris made no reply. He was trying hard to concentrate his mind upon the sweet and common things of life. He even thought of silk and St Paul's Churchyard and the faces of his partners in business.

'For you came all prepared to be caught,' he heard the other's voice like someone talking to him from a distance; 'your deeply introspective mood had already reconstructed the past so vividly, so intensely, that you were *en rapport* at once with any forces of those days that chanced still to be lingering. And they swept you up all unresistingly.'

Harris tightened his hold upon the stranger's arm as he heard. At the moment he had room for one emotion only. It did not seem to him odd that this stranger should have such intimate knowledge of his mind.

'It is, alas, chiefly the evil emotions that are able to leave their photographs upon surrounding scenes and objects,' the other added, 'and who ever heard of a place haunted by a noble deed, or of beautiful and lovely ghosts revisiting the glimpses of the moon? It is unfortunate. But the wicked passions of men's hearts alone seem strong enough to leave pictures that persist; the good are ever too lukewarm.'

The stranger sighed as he spoke. But Harris, exhausted and shaken as he was to the very core, paced by his side, only half listening. He moved as in a dream still. It was very wonderful to him, this walk home under the stars in the early hours of the October morning, the peaceful forest all about them, mist rising here and there over the small clearings, and the sound of water from a hundred little invisible streams filling in the pauses of the talk. In after-life he always looked back to it as something magical and impossible, something that had seemed too beautiful, too curiously beautiful, to have been quite true. And, though at the time he heard and understood but a quarter of what the stranger said, it came back to him afterwards, staying with him till the end of his days, and always with a curious, haunting sense of unreality, as though he had enjoyed a wonderful dream of which he could recall only faint and exquisite portions.

But the horror of the earlier experience was effectually dispelled; and when they reached the railway inn, somewhere about three o'clock in the morning, Harris shook the stranger's hand gratefully, effusively, meeting the look of those rather wonderful eyes with a full heart, and went up to his room, thinking in a hazy, dream-like way of the words with which the stranger had brought their conversation to an end as they left the confines of the forest.

'And if thought and emotion can persist in this way so long after the brain that sent them forth has crumbled into dust, how vitally important it must be to control their very birth in the heart, and guard them with the keenest possible restraint.'

But Harris, the silk merchant, slept better than might have been expected, and with a soundness that carried him halfway through the day. And when he came downstairs and learned that the stranger had already taken his departure, he realised with keen regret that he had never once thought of asking his name.

'Yes, he signed in the visitors' book,' said the girl in reply to his question.

And he turned over the blotted pages and found there, the last entry, in a very delicate and individual handwriting –

'*John Silence*, London.'

www.ingramcontent.com/pod-product-compliance
Lightning Source LLC
Chambersburg PA
CBHW030543180626
46810CB00005B/1983